# BAXTER,
## the Pig Who Wanted to Be Kosher

BY Laurel Snyder • ILLUSTRATED BY David Goldin

TRICYCLE PRESS
Berkeley

One fine day, when Baxter was waiting for his bus, an old man sat down beside him and said, "Oh, I wish it were sundown right now."

"Why's that?" asked Baxter. He was a curious sort of pig.

"Because at sundown," said the old man, "the candles gleam and glow and dance while our sweetest voices lift in song!"

"They do?" asked Baxter. He had never seen a candle dance.

"Certainly," said the old man. "Tonight is the beginning of Shabbat, the day of rest, and so we make a special dinner. We light the candles, sing our thanks, and raise a glass, surrounded by those we love best."

"Wow!" said Baxter. "That *does* sound like fun. That sounds terrific!"

"It *is* terrific," said the old man, as his bus pulled up. Then he was gone.

All week long Baxter thought about the old man's words.

"The candles gleam and glow and dance while our sweetest voices lift in song!"

So the following Friday, Baxter hurried back to the bus stop.

But the old man was nowhere to be seen. Instead, Baxter found a younger man wearing a long white apron.

After a while, Baxter cleared his throat. "Ahem! I wonder, sir, do you know anything about Shabbat dinner?"

"I should hope so," replied the man in the apron.

"Oh, good," said Baxter. "Will you tell me how I can be part of it?"

The man in the apron stared. "YOU? A pig? Part of Shabbat dinner? That's impossible!"

"Why?" asked Baxter.

"You're not kosher!" said the man in the apron.

"Kosher?" asked Baxter. "What's kosher?"

But just then the bus arrived.

That night, Baxter happened to be at the grocery store when he noticed a jar on the very top shelf.

"KOSHER" read the big block letters across the jar of pickles.

Why, Baxter loved pickles!

That week, Baxter ate pickles.
Pickles and pickles and pickles.

Pickle sandwiches
and pickle soup.

Pickles for breakfast and
pickles in bed.

On Friday, he arrived at the bus stop smelling of vinegar and lugging his jar. But this time, there was a woman in a large hat sitting on the bench. When Baxter sat down beside her, she wrinkled her nose and scooched away from him.

"What's with the pickle juice?" she asked.

"I found kosher," Baxter said proudly.

"Mazel tov," said the woman in the large hat. "So what?"

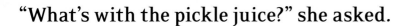

"So . . . ," he said. "Do you think *I'm* kosher yet?"

The woman in the large hat just laughed. "Pickles can dress up a sandwich or brighten a day. They're good, but they aren't *that* good."

Sadly, Baxter set down his jar.

The next day, Baxter returned to the grocery store.

"Excuse me, sir," he said to the store manager. "Do you have anything else kosher? The pickles were delicious, but I'm afraid they didn't quite do the trick."

The manager pointed Baxter toward an enormous pile of fresh bread.

Baxter had never tasted raisin challah before.

"Mmmmmmm . . ."

Five loaves later and sick to his little, round stomach, he moaned, "I must be kosher by now. Maybe even a little *too* kosher."

Later that day, Baxter arrived at the bus stop and found the old man had returned.

"Shalom," said the old man.

"Hello!" said Baxter. "I'm glad you're here! I've learned so much—all about pickles and challah! What do you think? Am I kosher yet?"

The old man looked puzzled.
"You want to be kosher?"

Baxter nodded.

"Well, now I've heard it all," said the old man. "But a pig is a pig is a pig. It's too bad you aren't a cow. *Cows* are kosher!"

All week long Baxter worked on his mooing. He acquired a handy set of horns. He cultivated a taste for clover.

By Friday, he felt fairly certain he was nearly bovine.

But this time when he got to the bus stop, nobody was there.

He waited and waited but nobody came. He mooed once more for good measure.

Finally, dejected, he took off his horns and let out a deep sigh.

But just then he felt a tap on his shoulder.

Looking up, Baxter found a woman with a big book standing above him.

The woman said, "Hello, I'm Rabbi Rosen. Can I help you?"

"Oh, I only wish you could!" blurted Baxter. "But I fear it's hopeless. 'A pig is a pig is a pig.' I'll *never* be kosher."

The rabbi gasped.
"Why on earth would
you want to be kosher?"

"I want to be kosher,"
explained Baxter, "so
that I can be part of
Shabbat dinner.

I gorged on pickles.

I stuffed myself with challah.

MOOOO

I mooed and grazed and wore
these silly horns for days!
But nothing's working!"

"But," said the rabbi, "why would you want to get eaten?"

"Eaten?! Me?" Baxter looked up sharply. "Who said anything about getting eaten?

I want to see the candles gleam and glow and dance. I long to lift my sweetest voice in song! Isn't that what Shabbat dinner is all about?"

The rabbi burst into laughter. "Yes, those things are important, it's true, but, my little pink friend, there has been a terrible misunderstanding. Although you're not kosher to eat and never will be, *everyone* is welcome at Shabbat dinner!"

Then the rabbi opened her book and rifled through it. "See," she said, "look right here. It is a mitzvah to welcome a stranger—and you, my friend, are certainly strange. So I'd be most grateful if you'd join me for Shabbat dinner tonight."

Baxter beamed. "Oh, thank you!" he said. "Thank you very much!"

And so at last Baxter the pig
watched the candles gleam
and glow and dance.

And so he raised his sweetest voice in song.

And he had a wonderful time.

Though it must be admitted he made rather a mess of his kugel.

*Dear nice reader,*

Jewish people love to invite strangers to supper! We've been doing it for thousands of years, ever since a guy named Abraham first started asking people into his tent to break bread. There's a fancy name for it—*hachnasat orchim*—but really the idea is pretty simple:

You make a new friend. You ask him to supper.

Best of all is asking someone over for Shabbat dinner. Because on Shabbat we stop working. We ignore our computers and our TVs and our phones. We light candles, make a nice meal, and pay attention to one another. We talk and listen and sing.

It's a holiday! Every week! How great is *that*?

You should try it sometime. If you're lucky, *your* stranger will help you clear the table!

(Unlike Baxter, who curled up and took a nap.)

## GLOSSARY

**challah** – scrumptious shiny, braided, golden bread, often with raisins nestled sweetly inside it. Traditionally served at Jewish holidays. Best when braided with your own two hands!

**kosher** – food that meets traditional biblical standards for Jewish munching is described as kosher. One important rule is that you can't mix milk and meat together (no cheeseburgers!). But a lot of these rules just tell you not to eat certain icky animals you wouldn't want to eat anyway. For instance, no fried vultures. And no roasted rats!

**kugel** – traditional Jewish casserole of sorts. There are many different kinds of kugel—some with noodles and apricots, and some with potatoes and onions. All are delicious.

**mazel tov** – literally "good luck" in Yiddish and Hebrew. But when someone says it, what they really mean is "congratulations!" Used, for instance, when someone wins a spelling bee.

**mitzvah** – good deed. Jews are commanded to follow lots of rules to help make their lives, and the world, better. There are 613 of these, some big and some little. You probably know tons of them already. At least ten!

**rabbi** – learned, generous Jewish leader who devotes time to reading, thinking, teaching, and helping people (and pigs!). Rabbis often tell wonderful stories, wear hats, and have nice laugh wrinkles.

**Shabbat** – Sabbath, day of rest. From sundown Friday until Saturday night (when three stars appear in the sky), Jews celebrate in different ways. Some families go to synagogue, and some spend the day doing fun things they don't have time for during the week, like bowling!

**shalom** – the Hebrew word for "hello." It also means "good-bye" and "peace" (like aloha). Fun to say!

SHALOM!

This book is dedicated to Jerry Sorokin, who offered me a place at the table.
But also, this book is dedicated to anyone who has ever felt excluded in any way.
Which is to say, this book is dedicated to everyone. —L.S.

To Rabbi Joyce Baraban Reinitz. —D.G.

Text copyright © 2010 by Laurel Snyder
Illustrations copyright © 2010 by David Goldin

All rights reserved.
Published in the United States by Tricycle Press, an imprint of Random House Children's Books,
a division of Random House, Inc., New York.
www.randomhouse.com/kids

Tricycle Press and the Tricycle Press colophon are registered trademarks of Random House, Inc.

Library of Congress Cataloging-in-Publication Data
Snyder, Laurel.
  Baxter, the pig who wanted to be kosher / by Laurel Snyder ;
illustrated by David Goldin.
    p. cm.
  Summary: When Baxter the pig hears about the joys of Shabbat
dinner he tries to become kosher so that he can participate.
[1. Sabbath—Fiction. 2. Kosher food—Fiction. 3. Pigs—Fiction. 4.
Jews—Fiction. 5. Humorous stories.] I. Goldin, David, ill. II. Title.

  PZ7.S6851764Bax 2010
  [E]—dc22
                          2009032293

ISBN 978-1-58246-315-5 (hardcover)
ISBN 978-1-58246-360-5 (Gibraltar lib. bdg.)
ISBN 978-1-58246-373-5 (PJ Library)

MANUFACTURED IN CHINA

Design by Colleen Cain

Type colophon in Jetsons and Eidetic Neo

The illustrations in this book were rendered in pen and ink and collage with digital enhancement.

071830.2K4/B1226/A6